This is a fiction work. Names, characters, places, and incidents are either the product of the author's imagination or used fictitiously. Any resemblance to actual people, living or dead, or actual events is purely coincidental.

Printed in the United States of America.

First Edition

ISBN: 979-8-9930012-6-5

For my grandkids. Your love inspires me every day. You remind me to slow down and notice, and love deeply.

Chapter One

The last bell of the year rang, and Emma stepped outside into warm air that smelled like cut grass and hot pavement. Summer.

She skipped down the sidewalk, her backpack thumping against her back, already thinking about long afternoons and friends she hadn't seen yet.

Halfway home, she slowed.

Tia, Sam, and Liz were standing near the corner, talking the way people do when they don't notice anyone else. Emma knew that sound, the easy laughter, quick words that didn't get stuck.

She stayed where she was, hoping they wouldn't look up.

Emma watched them and tried to imagine herself standing that way, speaking without planning every sentence.

"Emma!"

Liz's voice cut through her thoughts.

Emma's stomach tightened. She stepped forward anyway, careful with every movement, suddenly aware of the crack in the sidewalk and the way her shoelace felt a little loose.

"Come over here," Liz said, smiling.

Emma nodded, even though her heart was racing. She reminded herself to breathe. She reminded herself not to trip.

Emma smiled back, careful to keep it in place.

Up close, they all said hello at once, voices overlapping, laughing about summer plans that spilled out faster than Emma could follow. Camps. Sleepovers. A trip to the lake.

"You should come with us," Sam said.

"Yeah," Liz added.

"Yes," Emma said, before she had time to think.

The word surprised her as much as anyone else.

"That would be fun," she added, and this time she meant it.

They laughed again, the easy kind, and Emma laughed too. For a moment, it almost felt natural.

Almost.

The feeling didn't last. It never did.

The tightness returned, sudden and familiar, like a wave pulling back before it crashed. Emma kept smiling anyway. They walked together for a block before splitting off in different directions.

"See you later," Liz called, already turning away.

Emma waved, her arm lighter than it had been all afternoon.

She kept smiling as she walked. She couldn't help it. Her face felt warm, like something inside her had stretched awake.

She had been invited.

And she hadn't said the wrong thing. She hadn't tripped. She hadn't frozen.

The thought followed her all the way home, bright and humming. Emma replayed the moment in her head, the way the words had come out easily, the way no one had looked confused or impatient.

For once, everything had gone the way it was supposed to.

She smiled the entire walk.

She didn't notice when the smile started to feel tired.

Chapter Two

The house smelled like dinner when Emma stepped inside.

Her dad glanced up from the television. He lifted his chin once, then looked back at the screen.

Emma paused, waiting for something else.

Nothing came.

She walked past the living room toward the kitchen. Her mom stood at the stove, stirring without looking up.

"Put your things away," her mom said. "Then come sit at the table."

Emma nodded.

No one asked how her last day of school had gone. No one asked why she was smiling. No one asked where she had been walking from.

Emma went to her room and set her backpack down carefully, the way she did when she didn't want to make noise.

The excitement she'd been carrying all the way home shifted, settling somewhere quieter.

By the time she came back to the table, it felt like something she'd imagined.

They sat down at the table a few minutes later. Plates clinked softly as her mom set them down.

Emma picked at her napkin, then stopped.

"Something happened after school," she said.

Her dad muted the television. Her mom looked up.

Emma told them about seeing Tia, Sam, and Liz on the way home. About being invited to join them. About the plans that had already started tumbling out, camping, the lake, staying up late.

She laughed as she spoke, surprised by how easy the words felt once they started.

"That sounds fun," her mom said.

Her dad nodded. "Looks like you'll have a busy summer."

They laughed when Emma described how everyone talked at once, how no one could agree on what to do first. Emma laughed too, her shoulders loosening without her noticing.

Her mom reached over and rested a hand on Emma's shoulder. "You can invite them over sometime," she said.

Emma nodded, already imagining it.

Later, in her room, she stared at her phone for a long moment before pressing Liz's name.

When Liz answered, Emma's smile came back, quick and bright.

She went to bed that night feeling lighter than she had in a long time.

The feeling stayed with her as she fell asleep.

Chapter Three Emma woke to the sound of the front door closing hard. She sat up in bed, confused. Her dad never left early on
weekends. He stayed home. He made pancakes. He watched the news too loudly. She listened, waiting to hear something else. Nothing came. After a while, Emma got out of bed and got ready for the
day. The house felt different as she walked downstairs, quiet, as if it were holding its breath. Her dad stood by the window, staring out at the yard. His
hands were in his pockets. He didn't turn around when she reached the bottom step. "Good morning, Daddy," Emma said. He startled slightly, then turned and smiled at her. It wasn't
his usual smile. He crossed the room and pulled her into a hug, longer than he ever did. That was when Emma knew something was wrong. When her dad let go, she stayed where she was, watching
his face.

"Are you okay?" she asked.

He nodded once, then sat down on the couch. "Come sit with me."

Emma did. She folded her hands in her lap, the way she did when she didn't know what was coming next.

"I need to tell you something about Grandma," he said.

Emma's stomach tightened.

"She had a fall last night," he continued. "She's in the hospital."

"Is she okay?" Emma asked quickly.

Her dad didn't answer right away. He rubbed his hands together and looked at the floor.

"She hasn't woken up yet," he said. "Mom went to stay with her."

Emma sat very still.

"Can we go see her?" she asked.

"Not yet," her dad said. "The doctors are helping her. When she wakes up, we'll go."

Emma nodded, even though she didn't like how that sounded.

The phone rang.

Her dad pushed himself up from the couch so quickly that the cushions sank back out of place. He answered in the kitchen, his voice low. Emma could hear words but not sentences.

She looked at the doorway, waiting.

When he came back, his face looked different.

That scared her more than anything else.

"Is Grandma okay?" Emma asked.

He paused. Then he said, "I need you to go feed the dogs, okay? We'll talk later."

"What about Grandma?" Emma asked. "Was that mom"?

"Yes," he said softly. "We'll all talk when she gets home."

Emma didn't wait to hear anything else.

She ran outside, the cool air pressing against her cheeks. Dutchess lifted his head when he saw her, tail already wagging.

Emma dropped to her knees and wrapped her arms around him. He leaned into her, solid and warm.
She pressed her face into his fur and cried.

Dutchess stayed still, breathing slowly, as if he knew not to move.

When the tears slowed, Emma wiped her face and filled his bowl. She sat with him in the yard afterward, watching him eat.

The morning passed quietly.

Chapter Four

Emma stayed where she was, the grass cool beneath her legs.

Dutchess shifted in her lap, his head heavy and warm. She rested her hand on his neck and focused on the steady rise and fall of his breathing. It helped, just a little.

Her dad's words came back to her in pieces.

The hospital.
Not yet.
When she wakes up.

Emma stared at the yard without really seeing it.

The fence.
The tree.
The worn patch of dirt near the gate.

Everything looked the same as it always had. And yet, it didn't feel the same.

A sound broke the quiet.

Emma lifted her head.

At first, she thought it was just the wind moving through the leaves. The branches at the edge of the yard swayed, though the air around her felt still.

Dutchess's ears twitched.

Emma followed his gaze.

Something rustled near the far fence, quick and light. Not loud enough to be startling. Not quite enough to ignore.

She held her breath.

Nothing moved again.

Emma let out a slow breath she hadn't realized she was holding. She told herself it was probably a squirrel. Or a bird. The yard was full of small sounds she didn't usually notice.

Still, she kept watching.

The longer she sat there, the more she became aware of how quiet everything else was, the house behind her, the street beyond the fence, the afternoon stretching on without direction.

Dutchess shifted again, then settled, his weight steady against her legs.

Emma ran her fingers through his fur and stayed very still.

Whatever it was, it had disappeared.

But the feeling didn't leave either.

Emma stayed outside until the sun moved higher and the shadows changed shape around her. When she finally stood up, her legs felt stiff, like she'd been sitting longer than she thought.

Just before Emma turned back toward the house, she caught a glimpse of something rust-colored slipping between the tall grass near the fence, quick, quiet, and gone before she could be sure of it.

Chapter Five

Emma stood at the bottom of the stairs, her shoes already on.

Her dad was in the kitchen, staring at his phone like it might say something different if he looked long enough.

"Daddy," Emma said.

He turned. "Yes, sweetheart?"

"Can I go see Grandma?"

The question landed between them.

He didn't answer right away. He set the phone down on the counter and rubbed the back of his neck. "I don't know," he said finally. "It's a long day. And the hospital can be hard."

"I'll be quiet," Emma said quickly. "I won't get in the way."

That wasn't what he was worried about.

He looked at her for a long moment. Emma stood very still, her hands clenched at her sides. She didn't know why she felt like she needed to convince him — she just knew she did.

"I just want to see her," Emma said. "I want her to know I'm there."

Her dad let out a slow breath.

He felt helpless lately. Helpless watching his wife come and go, exhausted. Helpless, hearing updates he didn't understand. Helpless, standing in his own house, waiting.

Maybe this was something he could do.

"Okay," he said at last. "We can go for a little while."

Emma's shoulders dropped in relief.

On the drive, neither of them talked much. The road hummed beneath the tires. Emma watched the trees blur past the window, her reflection flickering in the glass.

Her dad kept both hands on the wheel.

When they pulled into the hospital parking lot, he turned the engine off and sat there for a moment.

"Remember," he said gently, "Grandma might not wake up. And she might not know you're there."

Emma nodded. "That's okay."

He studied her face, searching for something, fear, maybe, or doubt.

Instead, he saw resolve.

"Alright," he said. "Let's go."

Chapter Six

The hospital smelled different from anywhere Emma had ever been.

Clean, but sharp. Like the air had been scrubbed too hard.

She stayed close to her dad as they walked down the hallway, her footsteps quiet against the floor. People passed them without looking. Voices stayed low, like everyone knew this wasn't a place for loud sounds.

When they reached the room, her dad stopped and pushed the door open slowly.

Grandma lay in the bed, still and pale, machines blinking softly beside her. Emma froze for a moment, her chest tightening. This didn't look like the grandma who baked cookies and hummed while she worked.

Her mom stood near the bed, smoothing the blanket again, even though it was already straight.

Emma looked around the room.

That was when she saw Grandpa.

He stood near the window, his back to the bed, his hands folded in front of him. He didn't turn when Emma came in. He didn't seem to notice anyone at all.

Emma felt something pull at her.

She walked toward him slowly.

Grandpa looked down when he felt her there. His eyes were red. A single tear slid down his cheek before he could wipe it away.

Emma didn't speak. She reached up and took his hands in both of hers. They were warm. Strong. Trembling just a little.

Grandpa's fingers curled around her, squeezing gently, as if he was afraid to hold too tightly. He didn't let go.
They stood like that together.

Emma felt his hand shake once, then steady. She looked up at him, and he met her eyes. His gaze was tired. Sad. But kind. And full of something Emma didn't have a name for yet.

She stayed.

She didn't ask questions.
She didn't say she was sorry.
She didn't try to make it better.

She just stood there, holding her grandpa's hands.

After a while, Grandpa squeezed her fingers again, a little firmer this time.

Emma squeezed back.

Chapter Seven They stood in the hallway just outside Grandma's room. Emma's mom spoke first, her voice careful. "You don't have
to stay tonight," she said. "You can come home with us. Get some rest." Grandpa shook his head. "No," he said gently.

"My place is here." No one argued with him. He turned toward Emma then and slowly knelt, so they
were eye to eye. It took effort, and Emma noticed the way he steadied himself before resting on one knee. He looked at

her for a long moment. "Thank you," he said. He didn't explain what he meant.
He didn't have to.
He pulled her into a hug, strong and sure. Emma wrapped her arms around him and held on. She felt his breath against her shoulder, slow and steady now.

"I'll see you soon," Grandpa said.

Emma nodded. She smiled a little, even though her throat felt tight. She leaned forward and kissed his cheek.
"I love you," she whispered.

Grandpa closed his eyes for just a second before standing.

Emma walked down the hallway with her parents; her hand tucked into her dad's. When she looked back once more, Grandpa was already returning to Grandma's room.

He didn't look away.

Chapter Eight

The girls came over on a quiet afternoon.

Emma heard their voices before she saw them, familiar, careful, like they weren't sure how loud they were allowed to be. She looked up from the porch steps as Tia, Sam, and Liz walked up the path.

"Hi," Liz said, smiling.

Emma smiled back. "Hi."

They sat down with her, close enough that their knees almost touched. For a moment, no one said anything. Dutchess lay nearby, his head on his paws, watching.

"We wanted to see how you were doing," Sam said finally.

Emma shrugged, then stopped herself. "I'm okay," she said. It was true, and not true, all at once.
Liz nodded. "We were going to the lake tomorrow."

The words landed softly, but Emma felt them anyway.

"We didn't want to just leave without telling you," Tia said.
"But we also didn't want to make you feel bad."
"And we didn't want to lie," Liz added.

Emma looked down at her hands. She traced the edge of a crack in the porch step with her finger. She thought about Grandma. About Grandpa. About the quiet that had settled into her days.

Sam leaned forward a little. "We can stay," she said. "If you want."

"We really mean that," Liz said quickly. "We can go another time."

Emma felt something tight in her chest. For a moment, she wanted to say yes. She wanted them to stay. She wanted things to feel normal again.

But she thought about how hard it had been for everyone lately. Waiting didn't mean stopping.

She looked up.

"You should go," Emma said.

The girls froze.

"It's okay," Emma added. "I want you to."

"Are you sure?" Tia asked.

Emma nodded. "Yeah. I'll be here when you get back."

Liz reached over and squeezed her hand. "Okay," she said softly.

They sat together a little longer, talking about small things, the weather, school starting again someday, nothing important. When the girls finally stood to leave, Emma watched them walk down the path.

Emma got up again with Dutchess beside her. They went and sat at their usual spot on the grass.

Emma then noticed the grass was moving near the fence, slower this time.

A fox stepped into view.

She didn't come close. She didn't run.

She just stood there, watching, until Dutchess lifted his head.

Then she slipped back into the trees.

Emma smiled and told Dutchess it was a fox, and she was gone now. Dutchess lay back down with his head in Emma's lap.

Chapter Nine

Three weeks had passed since Grandma had been taken to the hospital.

Emma knew because she had started counting the days in her head. Not all at once. Just here and there, when the hours felt longer than usual.

She sat beside Grandma's bed, a book open in her lap. It was one of Grandma's favorites, the one with the soft blue cover and the worn pages that smelled faintly like dust and vanilla.

Emma read slowly, careful with each word.

Grandma didn't move. Her eyes stayed closed. The machines beside the bed blinked and hummed quietly, like they were breathing for her.

Emma didn't rush.

When she finished a page, she paused before turning to the next one, just in case.

She leaned closer and began again.

Outside the room, Emma's mom and dad stood together near the window. They watched her without speaking. Every so often, her mom folded her arms, then unfolded them again. Her dad rubbed his thumb along the edge of his phone, though he wasn't looking at it.

Grandpa sat in the chair by the bed.

He hadn't moved much since Emma arrived. His eyes stayed on Grandma's face, searching for something, no change at all.

Emma closed the book gently and rested it on the table.

"Grandma," she said softly, "I saw a fox today."

Her mom and dad glanced at each other.

Emma didn't notice.

"He comes out near the fence now," she continued. "He just sits there. Dutchess doesn't bark. He just watches." She shifted in her chair, keeping her voice calm and steady.

"I think he knows when to leave."

Grandpa's hand tightened slightly around the arm of his chair.

Emma looked over at him.

"He doesn't stay long," she added. "But he always comes back."

She picked up the book again and opened it to where she had left off.

"I'll read some more," she said.

Grandpa nodded without looking away from Grandma.

Emma began reading again, her voice quiet and even. She didn't know if Grandma could hear her. She didn't know if it mattered.

She read anyway.

Chapter Ten The knock came while Emma was sitting at the kitchen
table, turning a smooth blue stone again in her hands.
She looked up, surprised, then slid her chair back and walked to the door.
Tia, Sam, and Liz stood on the other side, sunburned and smiling, their hair pulled back in loose ponytails.
"Hi," Liz said.

Emma smiled. "Hi."

They stepped inside, suddenly quieter than usual, like they weren't sure how much space they were allowed to take.
"We brought you something," Sam said.

Tia held out a small paper bag, folded carefully at the top.

Emma hesitated, then reached for it.

Inside was another stone, pale blue like the one she already had, with a tiny white wave painted across it. The paint was slightly uneven, like someone had done it by hand.

"We found it near the lake," Liz said. "It made us think of you."
Emma turned the stone in her palm. It felt warm, like it had been held for a while before being given away.
"We talked about you a lot," Tia added. "We wished you were there."
Emma nodded. "I'm glad you went," she said. And this time, she meant it.

They moved to the living room and sat together on the floor, their backs against the couch. No one rushed to fill the quiet.

Sam glanced around. "How's your grandma?"

"She's still sleeping," Emma said. "But I read to her."

Liz smiled softly. "She's lucky."

Emma didn't answer. She didn't need to.

They stayed for a while, talking about small things, the long drive, the snacks they packed, how the water felt colder than it looked. Nothing felt forced. Nothing felt left out.

When the girls finally stood to leave, Emma walked them to the door. She watched as they headed down the path, the blue stone resting securely in her hand.

She closed the door gently behind her and stood there for a moment before turning back into the house.

Chapter Eleven Emma stood at the kitchen sink, rinsing out her cup. The girls' laughter still echoed faintly in her head, even
though they had already gone. She stared out the window longer than she meant to, her hands resting in the water.

She didn't notice her mom watching from the doorway. Her mom saw it, though. The way Emma's shoulders dipped. The way her smile faded once she thought she was alone. The sadness that passed across her face—quick, practiced, uncomplaining.
Emma dried the cup and set it upside down on the towel.

Her mom walked over and rested her hands on the counter beside her. "You've been doing a lot lately," she said gently.

Emma shrugged. "It's okay."

Her mom studied her for a moment. "I think you need a break."

Emma turned. "But Grandma"

"I know," her mom said. "And she's not going anywhere tonight."

Emma hesitated. She looked down at her hands. "What about Grandpa?"
"He'll stay with her," her mom said. "And I'll be back later."

Emma didn't answer right away.

Her mom smiled a little. "I already talked to Sam's mom," she added. "The girls are having a sleepover tonight. I thought you might want to go."

Emma's heart lifted before she could stop it.

Then it sank again.

"I should stay," she said. "In case you need help."

Her mom reached out and brushed a strand of hair behind Emma's ear. "Helping doesn't always mean staying," she said. "Sometimes it means letting yourself rest."

Emma searched for her face, looking for doubt. She didn't find any.

"You'll be back in the morning," her mom continued. "Grandma will still be sleeping. Grandpa will still be there. Everything will be okay."

Emma nodded slowly.

"Okay," she said.

Her mom smiled, relief and something softer crossing her face. "Go pack a bag."

Emma moved toward the stairs, then paused.

"I'll come back early," she said.

Her mom nodded. "I know you will."

Chapter Twelve

Emma burst through the front door the next morning, her overnight bag slipping off her shoulder.

"I'm back!" she called.

Her mom appeared in the hallway, smiling in a way Emma hadn't seen in a long time. It wasn't careful. It wasn't tiring.

It was bright.

"Get your shoes back on," her mom said.

Emma froze. "Why?"

Her mom crouched in front of her. "Because Grandma is awake."

For a second, Emma didn't understand the words.

Then they landed.

"She's awake?" Emma squealed.

Her mom laughed and gently held her shoulders. "Quiet excitement," she said. "We're going to the hospital."

Emma grabbed her shoes, her hands shaking as she tied the laces too fast, then too slow. Her heart felt like it was running ahead of her body.

The hospital didn't feel as heavy this time.

When they stepped into Grandma's room, Emma saw her eyes open, just barely, but open. Grandma's gaze drifted, unfocused, then settled for a moment.

Emma gasped.

"Grandma!" she shouted, her voice shooting straight out of her.

"Emma," her mom said quickly, laughing. "Inside voice."

Emma clapped her hands over her mouth, then pulled them away just long enough to talk.

"You're awake!" she said. "I had a sleepover, and I read to you, and I saw the fox again, and Grandpa stayed the whole time and..."

"Slow down," Grandpa said gently, smiling as he wiped his eyes. "One thing at a time."

Emma laughed, breathless, words tumbling over each other anyway.

Grandma blinked.

Her mouth moved, just a little.

Emma leaned closer, suddenly still.

Grandma's fingers twitched.

Emma felt it before she saw it.

"She's moving," Emma whispered.

"Yes," her mom said softly. "She's awake."

Emma bounced once on her toes before remembering where she was. She squeezed her hands together instead, her whole-body buzzing.

Everyone laughed, quietly, carefully, like they didn't want to scare the moment away.

Emma stood by Grandma's bed, smiling so wide her cheeks hurt.

She didn't need to say anything else.

Grandma was awake.

Chapter Thirteen

Grandma being awake didn't change everything all at once.

Emma learned that the next day.

When they returned to the hospital, Grandma's eyes were open again, but they didn't stay focused for long. Sometimes they drifted toward the ceiling. Sometimes they close without warning. Sometimes they rested on Emma's face for just a second too short to be sure.

Emma stood quietly beside the bed, her hands folded together.
"Good morning, Grandma," she said softly.

Grandma's mouth moved, but no sound came out.

Emma didn't rush her.

She pulled the chair closer and sat down, the legs scraping gently against the floor. Grandpa sat on the other side of the bed, his hand wrapped around Grandma's, the way it had been every day since she arrived.

"She's tired today," he said quietly.

Emma nodded. "That's okay."

Her mom stood near the window, talking with a nurse in hushed voices. Emma didn't listen to the words. She watched the nurse nod, the way her mom pressed her lips together afterward.
Emma looked back at Grandma.

"I can read," she offered.

Grandpa smiled faintly. "She likes that."

Emma opened the book she'd brought and began where she'd left off. Her voice stayed slow and even. She paused when Grandma's breathing changed, waited, then continued.

Grandma's fingers twitched.

Emma noticed.

She didn't say anything.

After a while, Grandpa leaned back into his chair, his eyes closing for just a moment. Emma kept reading anyway, holding the space the way she'd learned to do.

When the story ended, Emma closed the book gently.

"Do you want to stop?" her mom asked.

Emma looked at Grandma. Grandma's eyes were closed now, her face peaceful.

"No," Emma said. "I think she's just resting."

They stayed a little longer.

Later, when they walked back down the hallway, Emma felt tired in a new way. Not heavy. Just aware.

In the car, she watched the trees pass by and thought about how excited she'd been the day before. How she'd thought everything would be better right away.

She didn't feel disappointed.

She felt patient.

That afternoon, Emma went outside.

Dutchess followed her to the yard and settled beside her. Emma sat near the fence, the blue stone from the girls warm in her pocket.

The fox didn't appear.

Emma didn't mind.

She stayed anyway, watching the light change, listening to the quiet.
Some things came slowly.

She was learning how to wait.

Chapter Fourteen

Emma hadn't been to the hospital in a few days.

At first, it had been hard to stay away. Her cough wasn't bad, but it lingered, and no one wanted to risk Grandma getting sick. Emma understood, even though she didn't like it.

She missed the quiet room.
She missed reading aloud.
She missed sitting beside Grandpa.

By the third day, her cough was gone.

That morning, Emma woke up feeling lighter. Her chest didn't ache anymore. Her head felt clear.
"You're better," her mom said, touching Emma's forehead. "And I have something to show you."
Emma followed her down the hallway to the guest room.

The door was open.

The room looked different.

The bed had been made up of fresh sheets, the kind Grandma liked. A small table sat beside it, already cleared off. Against the wall, where the chair used to be, there was now a sofa that folded out into a bed.

"For Grandpa," her dad said from the doorway. "So, he can stay close."
Emma's eyes widened. "She's coming home?"

"Soon," her mom said. "Not today. But soon."

Emma smiled so wide her cheeks hurt. She walked into the room slowly, taking it all in. She
straightened the pillows, even though they were already neat. She smoothed the blanket, careful and gentle, as if Grandma were already there.

"I can help her," Emma said. "I can read to her. And bring her water. And…"

"I know," her mom said, smiling. "And we'll help too."

Emma nodded, her excitement settling into something steady.

Later, Emma carried folded towels into the room. She lined them up carefully on the dresser. She placed a book on the nightstand, one Grandma hadn't heard yet.

She felt useful.

She felt ready.

That afternoon, Emma sat on the floor of the guest room, leaning against the bed, imagining Grandma resting there. Grandpa is nearby. The house is full, but quiet.

Everything wasn't back to normal.

But it was moving forward.

And Emma was part of it.

Chapter Fifteen

Grandma came home in the late afternoon.

The house felt different the moment she arrived, full, but careful. Emma watched as her mom helped Grandma down the hallway, every step slow and deliberate. Grandpa stayed close, his hand never far from Grandma's arm.

They got her into the guest room, easing her into the bed Emma had helped prepare. Grandma sighed softly when she lay back, her eyes closing almost at once.

"She's exhausted," Emma's mom whispered.

"I can help," Emma said.

Her dad smiled at her. "That would be great. I'm going to get some clothes from Grandma and Grandpa's house."

When he left, Emma stayed close to her mom. She carried pillows, handed over water, and straightened blankets that didn't really need straightening. She moved quietly, careful not to wake Grandma.

When everything was finally done, the house fell still.

Grandma slept. Grandpa sat in the chair beside the bed, watching for her breathing.

Emma slipped outside.

The air felt cooler now, and the sun was lower in the sky. She sat near the fence, pulling her knees up to her chest, listening to sounds from the house behind her.

She stayed alert.

Just in case.

After a while, Emma looked toward the trees.

The fox wasn't there.

She scanned the yard, then the far edge where it usually appeared. Nothing moved. No rust-colored shape. No flicker of a tail.

Emma frowned slightly.

She hadn't seen the fox in days.

Dutchess lay beside her, his head resting on his paws. Emma reached out and scratched behind his ears.

"Maybe he's resting too," she whispered.

She stayed outside until the light faded, keeping one ear turned toward the house, ready to go back inside if she was needed.

The fox didn't come.

Emma didn't leave.

Chapter Sixteen

Emma was sitting on the edge of her bed when her phone buzzed.

She looked at the screen, Sam.

Her heart jumped before she could stop it.

"Hi," Emma said, keeping her voice quiet.

"We're going camping," Sam said. "My parents are coming. They're staying in the cabin by the lake. We'll be in tents right nearby."

Emma smiled, then hesitated. "When?"

"This weekend. Three days."

Emma glanced down the hallway toward the guest room. Grandma slept most of the afternoon. Grandpa sat beside her bed, reading quietly.

"I don't know," Emma said. "My grandma just got home."

"That's okay," Sam said quickly. "You don't have to come if you can't."

Emma held the phone a little tighter. "Can I ask my mom?"

"Of course."

Emma found her mom in the kitchen. She listened without interrupting as Emma explained, her words careful and measured.

"I want to go," Emma said finally. "But I don't want to leave Grandma if she needs me."

Her mom rested her hands on the counter. "Grandma will be okay," she said gently. "Grandpa and I will be right here. And I think this would be good for you."

Emma watched her face. "You're sure?"

Her mom nodded. "I wouldn't say yes if I wasn't."

Emma went back to her room and pressed the phone to her ear. "I can come."
Sam squealed so loudly that Emma had to pull the phone away.
The campsite was quieter than Emma expected.

Sam's parents stayed close, checking in often, but giving the girls space too. The trees stood tall around them, and the lake shimmered just beyond the path.

Emma felt lighter as soon as she stepped out of the car.

They spent the first afternoon setting up tents and gathering sticks. Emma laughed when Liz tripped over a root and pretended it was on purpose.

That night, they sat around the fire roasting marshmallows.

Emma stared into the flames for a long moment before speaking.

"I have something to tell you that I have never mentioned before," she said.
The girls looked at her.

"There's a fox near my house," Emma said. "I used to see him a lot."

"A fox?" Tia said.

Emma nodded. "He'd just sit there. Not close. Not far. He never scared Dutchess."

"Where is he now?" Liz asked.

Emma shrugged. "I haven't seen him in a while."

They all looked toward the trees, half-expecting to see something move.

"Maybe he went somewhere else," Sam said.

"Or maybe he's still around," Tia added. "Just watching."

Emma smiled.

Later, zipped into her sleeping bag, Emma stared up at the stars through the tent mesh. She thought about Grandma sleeping safely at home. About Grandpa nearby. About the fox, she hadn't seen.

Everything felt connected, even from far away.

Fun hadn't replaced responsibility. It had joined it.

Chapter Seventeen The next morning began quietly. Mist hovered over the lake, turning the water pale and still. Emma sat on a rock near the shore, her knees pulled to her chest, watching the surface ripple as something small moved beneath it.

"Cold," Liz said, dipping her toes in and jumping back.

Emma smiled. "It looks colder than it is."

Sam laughed. "That's not comforting."

They spent the morning skipping stones and walking along the edge of the lake, pointing out shapes in the clouds and arguing gently over who had the best throw. Emma surprised herself by winning once. She lifted her arms in triumph, laughing when the others groaned.

After lunch, Sam's parents suggested a short hike. The trail wound through tall trees, sunlight breaking through in soft patches. Emma walked near the middle of the group, listening more than talking, feeling steady and unhurried. At one point, the path narrowed, and they had to walk single file. Emma followed Liz, careful with her steps, noticing how the ground dipped and rose.

She didn't rush.

At the top of a small hill, they stopped to rest. Emma sat down on a fallen log and took a long drink of water. She looked out over the trees and felt something settle inside her.

Not excitement.

Contentment.

That evening, they built the fire again. The flames crackled softly, sending sparks into the darkening sky. Emma held her marshmallow just close enough to warm it, turning it slowly, the way she'd learned.

"This one's perfect," Sam said.

Emma grinned. "I know."

As night fell, they lay on blankets near the fire, counting stars. Emma named the ones she knew and made-up names for the rest. No one corrected her.

Later, zipped into her sleeping bag, Emma listened to the night sounds—the wind in the trees, the distant splash of something moving in the water.

She thought about home.

About Grandma resting in the guest room.
About Grandpa sleeping nearby.
About the fox, she hadn't seen it in days.

She wasn't worried.

She felt ready to go back.

The lake had given her what she needed.

Chapter Eighteen

Emma came home in the late afternoon.

The house felt warm when she stepped inside, like it had been waiting for her. Her mom was in the kitchen, humming softly as she stirred something on the stove.

"She's awake," her mom said before Emma could ask. "And she's feeling strong today."

Emma's smile spread slowly, like she didn't want to scare the moment away.

In the guest room, Grandma sat propped up in bed, a blanket across her legs and a book resting open in her lap. Grandpa stood nearby, talking quietly, his voice lighter than it had been in weeks.

"Emma," Grandma said.

Emma hurried to her side. "Hi, Grandma."

Grandma reached out and squeezed her hand. Her grip wasn't strong yet, but it was steady.

"I hear you've been busy," Grandma said with a small smile.

Emma laughed. "I went camping. And I helped Mom here. And I read to you even when you were sleeping."

Grandma nodded. "I heard."

They sat together for a while, talking slowly. Grandma tired easily, but she smiled often.

"The doctor says I'll be going home in a few weeks," Grandma said. "Still some healing to do."

"That's okay," Emma said. "We're good at waiting."

Later, Emma slipped outside.

Dutchess followed, stopping when she stopped.

The yard looked the same as always: the fence, the tree, the tall grass near the edge.

Then something moved.

Emma froze.

A familiar rust-colored shape stepped into view.

"The fox," Emma whispered.

She stood near the trees, thinner than Emma remembered, her movements careful. Behind her, two small shapes tumbled forward, clumsy and curious.

Then another.

And another.

Emma's breath caught.

"They're babies," she whispered.

The fox paused and looked back at them, then toward Emma and Dutchess. She didn't come closer. She didn't leave.

Dutchess tilted his head, ears forward, tail still.

Emma knelt slowly, keeping her movements calm.

"That's why you were gone," she murmured. "You were busy too."

The baby foxes stumbled through the grass, bumping into each other, stopping to sniff everything. One rolled onto its side and struggled to right itself.

Emma smiled, her chest warm.

She didn't reach out.

She didn't speak again.

She just watched.

After a while, the fox gathered her babies with a soft movement and led them back toward the trees. The last one glanced back once before disappearing.

Emma stayed kneeling long after they were gone.

Dutchess sat beside her, alert and quiet.

Life hadn't stopped while she waited.

It had been growing.

Chapter Nineteen

Emma noticed it in the afternoon.

Grandpa hadn't left the guest room all day.

He sat beside Grandma's bed, his hand resting over hers, his eyes fixed on her face. Grandma slept peacefully, her breathing slow and even. The room was quiet, the curtains pulled back just enough to let in soft light.

Emma stood in the doorway for a moment, watching.

"Grandpa," she said gently.

He looked up. "Yes, sweetheart?"

"She's sleeping," Emma said. "The nurse said she needs rest."

"I know," Grandpa said. He didn't move.

Emma stepped closer. "You do too."

Grandpa smiled faintly, but his eyes stayed tired. "I'm fine."

Emma hesitated. This part felt harder than she expected.

"Will you come sit outside with me?" she asked. "Just for a little while."

Grandpa looked back at Grandma, then at Emma. "I don't want to be far."

"We won't be," Emma said quickly. "Just the yard."

He was quiet for a long time.

Finally, he nodded.

Outside, the late afternoon sun warmed the grass. Emma led Grandpa to the bench near the fence. He sat down slowly, letting out a breath he didn't seem to realize he'd been holding.

They didn't talk right away.

Emma rested her hands in her lap, her eyes scanning the far edge of the yard. Grandpa followed her gaze.

"What are you looking for?" he asked.

Emma leaned closer and lowered her voice. "The fox."

Grandpa raised an eyebrow. "A fox?"

"She lives near the trees," Emma whispered. "She has babies."

Grandpa smiled, not the polite kind, but the kind of smile that reached his eyes. "That sounds like quite a thing to see."

"It is," Emma said. "She hasn't come back yet."

They sat quietly, watching.

The grass moved in the breeze. A bird fluttered past. Somewhere, a door closed softly inside the house.

Emma glanced at Grandpa. He looked calmer now, his shoulders lower, his breathing slower.

"It's okay if she doesn't come today," Emma said. "Sometimes she just watches from far away."

Grandpa nodded. "Sometimes that's enough."

They stayed there until the light began to fade.

The fox didn't appear.

But Grandpa stood a little taller when they went back inside.

And Emma smiled, carrying the secret with her.

Chapter Twenty

The house has settled into a new rhythm.

Grandma rested more than she moved, but every day she stayed awake a little longer. Grandpa no longer stayed in the chair beside her all the time. Sometimes he made tea. Sometimes he sat by the window, watching the yard.

Emma noticed.

That afternoon, Grandma was sitting up in bed, a blanket across her legs, her eyes clear. Emma sat beside her, turning the pages of a book slowly, careful not to rush.

Across the room, Grandpa stood at the window.

He had been quiet for a long time.

"Well," he said softly.

Emma looked up. "What is it?"

Grandpa leaned forward just a little. "I think I see something."

Emma slipped off the bed and walked over. Grandma shifted slightly, watching them.

Near the far edge of the yard, where the grass grew tall, a rust-colored fox stepped into view. Smaller shapes followed her, tumbling clumsily through the grass.

"Oh," Emma whispered. "Her babies."

Grandpa smiled, his eyes shining. "So that's where she's been."

The fox paused, just long enough to look back at the house. The babies bumped into one another, curious and unsteady. Then, just as quietly, they disappeared into the trees.

Grandpa stepped back from the window, shaking his head slightly, like he wanted to make sure he would remember it. Emma turned.

Grandma was smiling.

"I remember you telling me about her," Grandma said softly. "You said she watched from far away."
Emma nodded. Grandma reached out and squeezed her hand.
Later, Emma went outside.

Dutchess followed and lay down near the fence, his chin resting on his paws. Emma sat beside him in the grass, and the evening air cooled against her skin.

She didn't wait for anything.

She didn't listen to the movement.

She just sat.

Behind her, Grandpa laughed quietly at something Grandma said. The sound drifted through the open window, warm and steady.

Emma rested one of her hands on Dutchess's head and breathed in the moment.

Life had slowed down enough for her to notice things she might have missed before.

Not everything happened the way she expected it to, but that didn't mean something good wasn't growing anyway. Emma was home, happy in a quiet way, and satisfied with where she was.

The End

www.ingramcontent.com/pod-product-compliance
Lightning Source LLC
Chambersburg PA
CBHW050430110726
47899CB00008B/2921